FATE FOR THE SPACE COWBOY

MATCH MADE IN SPACE

PHOEBE BELLE

Chapter One

ROMI

Every breath hurts with the heat searing my lungs as I run. Dust kicks up all around as the horses race ahead of me. I hear a shout in the distance, sending a jolt of fear through me.

The fear galvanizes me, giving me another burst of adrenaline to run just fast enough. My favorite horse, Fury, slows his pace, circling beside me. I catch his mane and fling myself onto his back, holding on as he dashes ahead.

When I hear another shout, it's much more distant. The fear still burns through me. I need to get to safety. Fury gallops fast enough to catch up to the other horses. Blessedly, we cross the barrier, and I tap the tiny receiver hiding in the pocket of my worn pants.

The fence is electrified behind us now, so I start to relax inside. The entire herd keeps moving in unison. They know where to go to find safety. Long minutes later, they finally slow, turning into the gate for their pasture and their barn, a refuge.

I slide off Fury's back once he stops. He curls his neck around me as his nostrils flare with his heaving breath. "Thank you," I whisper. "Go." I release his mane.

He ambles over toward the large water trough. The only reason these horses have water is because we're near the green zone, with access to an aquifer. I'm not lucky enough to live in the green zone, but I'm lucky enough to be gifted at training horses. They answer to me; therefore, the ruling families of the green zone want me to help care for them.

I shield my eyes from the burning sun with my hand as I look out over the pasture behind me. We're by the ocean here, and the horses feed off the marsh grasses. This part of Earth is near the Outer Banks on the coast of the Atlantic Ocean. Horses survived shipwrecks from centuries ago and have lived here ever since. They've also survived the near destruction of the Earth. They're sturdy and strong.

My thoughts spin to my plan. Rumors about a matchmaking service for women have been racing through the area. I hope to convince the alien cowboys to take the horses with them. If humans can survive on that planet, so can horses.

That night, I return to what passes for home. They might want me to use my skills to help with the horses, but the ruling families don't want me to live too close to the green zone. Only the rich get that.

I don't even turn on a light, slipping in unnoticed through the back entrance and walking on quiet feet to the apartment where I grew up. Two rooms are a luxury here on Earth when you're poor. The funny thing, though, is that technology still works here. It's the one thing that Earth has not failed at. I pick up my smartphone. It's old and battered, and I don't carry it with me because I know there's a beacon in it. I tap it open and scroll through, looking for any news about the matchmaking service.

When my eyes land on another posting for interviews tomorrow, I debate whether I have the nerve to try. I know I'm not the best candidate. I'm tall, and I'm told that I'm too standoffish and intimidating for men. I don't care. Men here think they own women, and I guess they do.

The only way I've learned to avoid them is to be a complete bitch. After both of my parents died in a factory fire, I kept my head down and quietly continued working with the horses. I'm so grateful to have that job. The horses are the only things that have held me back from applying to the matchmaking service sooner. I fear leaving them behind.

Hours later, I hear the thumping on the door. I stare at it in the darkness.

"I know you're in there, Romi."

I want to ignore it, but I'm tired of letting my fear ruin my life. I sleep in my clothes as I always have. My mother taught me to do that. She always said it's the only way to stay safe at night. I stand, striding across the dark room to fling the door open.

I reach forward and grab Draven by the balls. "You fucking asshole. What do you want?" I demand.

His face is red under the dull light in the hallway, and he lets out a sharp grunt. I don't let go and twist his balls in my grip.

"You marry me." He thinks he can order me around. "In three days, I'll be back," he chokes out before he breaks free from my hold, stumbling down the hallway.

The next day, I feed the horses and use the shower in the barn. I twist my hair into a braid and study myself in the mirror. Although Earth is a dry and dusty hellscape, with most of us living in poverty and working for factories or massive offices, some manage to get by with nice clothes and cute things that they scrounge up from old storage garages. I haven't even bothered to find anything nice. I'm too practical.

I hope I'll get accepted anyway. Walking down the dusty road to Space Rodeo Drive, I feel him before I hear him. Draven stops beside me. "Two days," he says, his eyes dark.

Fear churns in my gut, but I don't even answer. A short while later, a woman named Jane looks at me. "Today," she says.

"We leave today?" I prompt.

She nods. For a split second, I almost lose my courage. But I have a promise to keep, a promise I made to myself and to my horses. I swallow nervously. "Can I ask you something?"

"Of course," she says. Jane is beautiful. I'm told she's the princess on this planet, but she insisted I call her Jane.

"Um, I take care of the horses here, the ones by the ocean. Is there any way at all that they can be brought to the planet? I know it's crazy that I'm asking, but..." I feel silly saying this. "They're like my family, and I don't want to leave them."

Jane is quiet for a few beats. She reaches over and clasps both of my hands, squeezing them gently. "Let me see what we can do." A moment later, she hurries away and returns with a tall, imposing man. "This is Asher, our prince."

The alien cowboy looks at her, his tail twitching. "*Your* prince," he says.

Jane's cheeks turn pink. "Can we bring the horses?"

He nods. "We can. Today, we are in a transport ship, so there is room. They will have to live with our horses, descended from earthly horses and dragons that went extinct on our planet. How will we get them to the ship?" he asks me.

"They'll follow me," I say.

Chapter Two

ROMI

Months later

I don't dare talk about my fear now that I'm here. It's been months since I arrived, and I have yet to meet a mate. I'm one of the original four women who traveled to this planet with Jane.

Nadine and Melody are happily married. Like Jane, they have the infinity pulse, this mythical thing where they're supposed to feel so connected to someone that it's instant and overpowering. Every time I think of it, I mentally scoff. Mostly because the idea of it frightens me a little.

Meanwhile, even though Jane assures me they will never send me back to Earth, I'm afraid. The alien cowboys from this planet did me a huge favor and let me bring the horses here. I worry they will banish me back to Earth. If that happens, I'll lose everything, even my horses.

Kicking those thoughts away, I walk out to the pasture. I care for the horses from this planet now, along with the horses from Earth. I'm so grateful they gave me this job. My favorite horse, Fury, comes racing over. He stops in front of me, dipping his head to press it against my chest. He lets out a snorting sound as I stroke behind his ears. Even though we don't speak the same language, I swear we're communicating. I believe he's telling me that he likes it here, that they all like it here.

"I do too," I whisper before dropping my forehead to his and breathing in the scent of hay and grass. This planet might be entirely different from Earth, but it shares many characteristics with how it was before humans nearly destroyed it. I suppose that's why humans originally came here centuries earlier. Our ancient cowboys, known for their love of travel, came here and stayed. It's why they can mate with us, why we can live here, and why the animals from Earth can also survive here.

My efforts to keep my anxieties at bay are failing. I'm afraid to talk about so many things right now, so they spin like annoying bees in my thoughts. A ship from Earth came here and is shaking things up because the planet is recruiting human women for mates. Of course, the men from Earth are idiots and don't even understand why women would jump at the chance to move to a new planet. Earth is a miserable place to be, and it relies on this planet and many other planets for food and supplies. That's the only leverage the leadership here has over the people from Earth.

"They won't take you back," I say to Fury.

Fury lifts his head and nudges me with his velvety-soft nose. This horse understands me. He knows I'm worried, and his affection eases my tension. After one more nudge, he twitches his tail and canters off. I'm walking back toward the stables when a prickle races down my spine, and I feel as if someone is watching me. I spin around, carefully scanning the area. Having been born and raised on Earth and having my parents identified as part of the resistance when I was a young girl, my instinct is to constantly be on guard.

While I feel much safer here, I don't believe anywhere is completely safe. They treat women amazingly well here. In fact, they worship them. But there is no perfect world, and our very princess, the one who has become a friend to me and is so incredibly kind, was kidnapped. She's been rescued and is safe again, but that event is a rupture in the fabric of kindness here. A small contingent of men would like this planet to be more like Earth. They want to rule over women. So I keep an eye out even though they swear a shield over this entire town protects us. I figure one can't be too careful.

As I turn back toward the stables, I see a horse approaching with his rider. The horse's name is Silver to match his coat, and he's gorgeous. I adore him. He only allows one alien cowboy to ride him, but I've never seen the man who rides him. I haven't been here whenever he has come to take Silver for a ride. I feel this alien cowboy watching me as I walk. On his own, Silver is imposing, and his rider sits tall, his tail draped along Silver's flank.

I feel a tug in my body, the sensation powerful in my heart and my belly. It feels as if a cord connects me to this alien cowboy. As he approaches, the cord feels as if it's literally tightening. All I want is to get closer. I shake the feeling away. I don't want to experience an infinity pulse. Its power frightens me. I don't want to be that connected to someone.

I'll be worried about being vulnerable, and I don't need that. I just need to marry and be treated decently. That's all I ask.

Chapter Three

THORNE

Silver snorts, bowing his head and ruffling his large wings slightly. Our horses here are similar to earthly horses, but they also have wings. I stroke a palm down the side of his neck. "Thank you for today," I say.

He curves his neck toward me, his eye meeting mine before he twitches his tail. I leave him in his spacious stall, where he will rest and eat like the spoiled creature he is. Only then do I give in to the urge humming inside me. I follow the tug I feel into the barn. Romi is there.

Moments later, I can still taste her on my mouth as she holds my gaze, lifting her chin. One kiss nearly brings me to my knees. As strong and stubborn as she tries to appear, I can feel her vulnerability shimmering under the surface. I feel her fear and almost disbelief that anyone can protect her.

"I promise I will protect you. Always. You must believe me," I say, my voice low.

A pink flush stains her cheeks, and her tongue darts out to slide across her bottom lip. The sight of it buries the claws of need even deeper into me. I never doubted the existence of the infinity pulse, but even then, its power takes me by surprise.

My parents loved each other deeply. When we lost my father,

my mother grieved so powerfully that I feared for her. She has recovered but insists she can be with no other man. Yet I hear the subtle shake in her voice and see the tremble in her hands when she speaks of my father. I worry for her often. It's only her strength that lets me know she will be okay.

"Who hurt you?" I ask Romi.

While I do not know who hurt her, I know she has been hurt deeply. A single tear slides down her cheek. I step closer, wrapping her in my embrace. I hope my touch conveys what I know in my heart and soul, that she will always be safe with me. "I will keep you safe," I rasp.

Romi stiffens for a beat before she softens against me, one arm sliding around my waist while the other palm presses against my heart. After a long moment, she lifts her head. I want to kiss away the tears streaked on her cheeks.

"You will, won't you?" she asks.

"Always," I promise.

The sound of horses running outside reaches us. "I have to take care of the horses," she says.

Reluctantly, I press a kiss on her forehead before stepping away. "I will talk to the prince and princess about our wedding. Until then, I will see you here every day."

Chapter Four

THORNE

"As you know, my princess will make all the arrangements." My longtime friend, and our planet's prince, lifts his chin, studying me quietly. "I'm happy for you. You deserve this." He reaches for my hands, clasping them both before he pulls me into a back-slapping hug.

Just then, there is a knock on his office door. "Yes?" Asher calls.

The door opens to reveal Hunter and Kayden standing on the other side. "Don't we have a meeting now?" Kayden asks.

"Oh, yes," Asher replies. "But first, I must share that Thorne has met his mate." His brows rise before a grin stretches across his face.

Like me, Kayden and Hunter are part of the security team for the royal family. While our planet is a democracy, we have royal leadership and protect them with our lives. Our families have been protectors of the royal family for generations, and we grew up together knowing this would be our calling.

After congratulations, the questions come. "Who is she?" Hunter asks with a brow waggle and a sly twitch of his tail.

Our kind have descended from the original humans on Earth who traveled here and mated with our ancestors. Our species is now a combination after centuries of mating. We have bronze skin and tails, dark golden hair, and golden eyes. We are slightly taller than the average human, as our original species was larger. Like much of the galaxy, we have traveled widely, mating with those species we can and establishing trade for supplies and technology.

Our planet is one of the wealthiest, and we serve as the central way station for travel among our galaxy. We worship the women here, which is why we are so strong. Many died in a space storm a few years ago, and we are desperate for mates. Asher hatched a plan to go to Earth and find his own princess. After that success, they are bringing more and more women from Earth to mate with our men. Earth is a dry, hellish place to live, and they hate women. Earth relies on us, along with a few other planets, to keep them limping along. They may not like us bringing women here, but they cannot stop it.

My friends have already mated and been teasing me that I'm too picky. I glance among them. "I was just waiting for my mate," I reply to Hunter. "It's Romi. She came with the first group the princess brought."

"And you hadn't met her yet?" Kayden prompts.

Asher chuckles and leans his hip against his desk. "Thorne is foolish and proud and didn't spend enough time at the gatherings to notice her. They met at the stables. As picky as Thorne is about Silver, Romi is the first, other than him, who can care for Silver."

Kayden chuckles. "Ah, so we're following the opinions of your horse."

"Silver trusts her, and he trusts few," I point out.

Hunter lets out a snort and nudges me with his shoulder. "Since you wouldn't take our advice, you might as well go with Silver's counsel. He's an excellent judge of character. Romi and Melody are close, so we'll see each other often."

Kayden rolls his eyes. "You already see each other every day unless we're out in the field or on missions."

Hunter shrugs easily. "It will make Melody happy for you to be mated to her friend. She says Romi has been worried she'll get sent back to Earth if she doesn't mate soon enough."

"Never." Asher slides his eyes to mine. "Even if she hadn't found a mate, she wouldn't have been sent back. We take care of our women here, and she is one of us now."

My heart thumps hard in my chest. "I will protect her now because she is mine."

"Oh, goddess! Grumpy Thorne has fallen," Kayden teases.

"You're gonna be the crankiest mate of all of us," Hunter adds.

I shrug away my friends' teasing, unperturbed. This isn't the first time I've been called grumpy, cranky, or broody.

"I'll tell Jane tonight so she can begin the wedding planning," Asher says.

Chapter Five

ROMI

Princess Jane lifts a glass, her smile encompassing the group of women. "It's Romi's turn. To happiness for you," she says.

We clink our glasses together, and I take a swallow of the decadent lemonade. Those of us here from Earth are still nearly giddy about the simple pleasures of drinking something other than the rationed and often dirty water available on Earth. The lemonade flavor is tart and sweet, and I love it.

Nadine smiles at me as she sets her glass on the table. "What's your favorite?" she asks.

"Our favorite what?" Melody prompts.

"Pink lemonade," I say.

Nadine nods. "That's what I mean, your favorite drink."

"But they're all amazing," I add.

"I'm partial to the pink lemonade as well," Jane offers with a smile.

"Well, Princess," Nadine replies with an arched brow. "You should make it the official planetary drink."

Jane rolls her eyes. "That seems silly."

"But why?" Melody prompts.

"And please stop calling me princess. It seems silly because that's an Earth thing. We were always naming things, most of them long gone. Ever since I got here, I think a lot about how sad it must've been on Earth for those who watched us lose everything once beloved there," Jane says, sadness flickering in her eyes.

The moment suddenly feels serious. Taking a quick breath, I clear my throat. "My grandmother remembered. She told me about when the storms got really bad before the rain stopped altogether. After that, she said the dryness began spreading everywhere."

We look around at each other. I've been here on this new planet for months now, and I still feel twinges of guilt for all the human women stuck on Earth. I feel so lucky that Jane selected me. Having food, clothing, shelter, and simple kindness feels beyond luxurious. It's such a dramatic change from the scraping-by and fear-filled life I led on Earth. Rationed food and water, threats and monitoring. Technology was the one thing they didn't let go of. Somehow, it was decided that they had to keep producing that, no matter how much it took from actual life. We all had our little smartphones, and some people even had computers. People who worked in the offices dressed nicely. We also had alcohol—anything to numb us from reality.

In hindsight, what happened was shocking. They tried to hide it. History books were destroyed. Some families saved them and hid them away. My grandmother kept a little stash of books about Earth before it all went to hell and before women became close to slaves.

"I'm sorry," I say, my words slipping out unbidden.

"For what?" Nadine prompts. She unconsciously slides her hand over her very round belly. She's pregnant again.

"I don't know. Everything got serious," I reply.

Jane lets out a little sigh. "We all know what life was like on Earth. Nadine and I worked in the offices, and I felt lucky. As much as I love it here, it makes me sad for Earth. I also see how it happened there," she says softly.

Nadine's eyes arc around the table. We're at her house

tonight. All of the beautiful homes on this planet are clean and spacious. I'm still in the extra house on the royal property with more women from Earth who have traveled here with the matchmaking service. This group of women is the one I've known the longest. Of them, I'm the last one to find my mate.

"Of course we see how it happened. A small contingent of bitter men," I say.

"Isn't it always bitter men who ruin worlds?" Nadine muses.

A flicker of fear zaps through me. "How worried is the Royal family about the protesters here?" I ask.

Jane takes a swallow of her lemonade before letting out another sigh. "Asher says it will be okay, but I know he worries. They all do."

I glance around at my friends. "What is it like to have your mates travel? Thorne will be traveling as well."

Nadine's lips curl in a soft smile. She's so pretty with her blond hair and blue eyes. I feel a sense of warm affection whenever I look at her. She's all soft and kind. She's also from a family of fighters on Earth, which is such a contrast to how she looks. I love that about her. "I always miss Kayden when he travels, but it makes it even better when he comes home," she says, her cheeks turning pink.

I feel a flush rise inside, heat suffusing my body. This infinity pulse that they've all talked about is startling to me. Ever since arriving here, I've told myself I only want to be safe. I've been more comfortable with the idea of mating without the infinity pulse. It seems less frightening. I didn't expect to experience this intense connection.

"Thorne is one of the most elite bodyguards on the security team and the most skilled rider of them all, according to Asher," Jane says. "I feel like Nadine. I miss Asher when he's gone, but it makes it all the better when he's here. His absence keeps it fresh in my mind and heart just how much he means to me."

"Exactly that," Melody says softly.

"How are you feeling about the wedding?" Jane asks.

I take a gulp of lemonade before setting the empty glass on the table. "Nervous, so nervous." I twist my hands together.

My friends collectively smile. "You're going to love it. Kayden says Thorne is very impatient," Nadine says with a sly glint in her eyes.

My lips curve in a nervous smile, and my belly flips.

———

Departing from Nadine's house, I walk along the flowered walkway with Melody.

I can't imagine I will ever become accustomed to the lush greenery here. Earth used to have areas like this—lush and beautiful rainforests, mountains, lakes, and streams. They are all gone now.

We make our way down the center street of town. This is a bustling area with stores, cafés, and more. Many residents walk, but some also use hovering transport vehicles that glide over the ground. As I look around, my lips curl into a smile. It still startles me to see how many different aliens live here. There are the alien cowboys with their bronze, shimmery skin and tails; tall, towering orcs; humans; and other aliens I don't even recognize. Almost everyone here is kind. It's remarkable how having everyone's basic needs met creates a sense of peace. Life on Earth is a scramble and fight for everything.

"I love it here so much," Melody says. She stops to pick a flower from a tree. She tucks it behind my ear, her eyes twinkling. "It suits you, Romi."

"I'm not really a flower type of girl," I say, feeling a little shy.

"Oh, but you are," she teases. "Your wedding next week will have lots of flowers. Are you ready?"

A sense of anxiety buzzes inside me. Ever since Thorne told me we were marrying, I've been anxious. I swallow nervously. "I am, but I'm not."

Melody stops walking, turning to face me and placing her

hands on my shoulders. "You're going to love it. Hunter says he's never seen Thorne like this. He says Thorne might be a little grumpy, but he's a good man and will take the best care of you. I promise you it will be better than you can imagine."

I take a shaky breath. "Okay, I believe you." My breath rushes out. "I just want to get through it so I don't have to worry about leaving the planet."

Melody squeezes my shoulders firmly before pulling me into a quick hug. "You won't have to leave the planet! Asher has assured us that no one who comes here from Earth will ever have to leave. They'll take care of us." The glint in her eyes turns teasing and sly. "And within a week, you'll be mated. Thorne is your fate. I know you're nervous, but I promise, you will love being with him."

Melody steps back, waving before she hurries into the flower shop where she works. I pass the coffee shop where Nadine works and wave at Trudy, the orc who manages it. She's outside, tending to the flowers she's planted in front of it. I keep walking before turning down the lane leading to the stables. My pulse quickens as I approach. Because the last time I was here, Thorne kissed me.

Chapter Six

ROMI

Every time I walk into the stables now, I think about Thorne and the way it feels to be near him.

Moments later, I stride into the supply room, where Thorne lit my body on fire with a kiss. There's no reason for me to think he will be here. Yet disappointment shoots through me when he's not. I swallow through the burst of emotion that rises. I don't need to be sad about not seeing an alien cowboy who kissed me. Even if I had never imagined feeling like that. Even if we have the infinity pulse.

Fortunately, I love my job, so I lose myself in work. I spend time training Fury and checking on the horses from Earth before shifting my attention to the other horses. If you'd told me on Earth that horses from there would mate with what were once dragons from here, I'd have laughed. They look mostly like horses now, but their fur shimmers in colors, and their wings are almost feathered in a more leathery way. They are intense and powerful. I've ridden a few of them, but I've yet to fly.

"Someday," I whisper to one of the female horses. Her name is Sasha. She's young and spunky. The elderly woman who runs the stables has told me Sasha hasn't been trained yet.

A while later, I'm preparing the evening feedings for the

young girl who comes out to handle those after I leave when awareness prickles up my spine. The hairs rise on the back of my neck, and my entire body vibrates in anticipation. Without seeing him, I know Thorne is here.

I try to order my pulse to slow, but it ignores me, dashing off at a breakneck pace, my heart beating so fast my breath is shallow. I hear footsteps coming down the walkway between the stalls. They rarely keep the animals inside here, but they all have places to rest.

"Romi."

Thorne's voice reaches me, echoing through my body like the reverberations from the ring of a bell. I turn to find him standing in the doorway, his shoulder propped against the frame.

His golden gaze locks with mine, and I could swear a flame licks through the air between us. When his eyes sweep up and down my body, I feel the heat of his fiery gaze in my belly. I shift restlessly on my feet, feeling the arousal slippery between my thighs. I'm not familiar with this sensation, and it's intense.

"Hi." My voice comes out breathless.

I mentally chastise myself. *Don't be silly. Get a grip.*

Thorne pushes away from the door and steps into the room, closing it behind him. The click of the latch echoes in the quiet space. I take a shallow breath, my senses absorbing the scents of this room—leather, hay, and grain, the familiar scent of horses. Dust moats float in the air, illuminated by the sunlight casting at an angle through the windows high on the wall.

"I was hoping I'd see you today." I can feel the low rumble of Thorne's voice in my body. He takes a step closer, his eyes never once breaking from mine.

"I'm here almost every day," I rasp.

He closes the distance between us in two strides, and my hips bump against a wooden counter that runs the length of the wall.

"A week," he says simply.

I can only nod because I don't trust myself to speak.

"Can I kiss you?" he asks.

My head bobs in another nod as I blink. His presence is an electric force as he stops immediately in front of me. His touch is light when he lifts his hand to palm my cheek. There's a gentle quality to it, yet his strength feels as if it surrounds me. The voltage of our connection shimmers around us.

I study him, taking in the bronze shimmer of his skin, which isn't quite scaled but almost looks as if it is. His presence is so powerful. It feels as if he is encompassing me. His golden eyes are intense, his features stark and bold. It's as if everything that makes a man in the human sense is taken up several notches with strong bones, a square jaw, and sensual lips. He towers over me, and it feels as if his eyes themselves are beams of light into the very heart of me.

It's as if he can see those old fears inside me, the loneliness I have carried for too many years. Beyond his shimmering electric force, I sense the natural intimacy between us. The tug of it is so strong that it's discombobulating.

His thumb strokes along the line of my jaw. His touch is warm, and I feel shockingly alive. I'm so hot, I imagine sparks leaping from my skin. His touch is a balm to my unsettled state. His thumb moves in a sensual caress over my bottom lip.

Unbidden, my mouth parts, and I try to breathe. I draw in the smallest sip of air. All the while, my heart rampages in my chest.

His gaze darkens. "Romi," Thorne whispers gruffly.

"Yes?" I whisper.

"You are my fate." His declaration rings in my heart.

Thorne's words set my racing pulse careening along faster and faster. Time feels simultaneously slow and fast as he bends low to bring his lips to mine. The moment our mouths collide, it's like lightning strikes between us, the air snapping with the burning-hot jolt of our connection.

His lips brush over mine, once and then again, before he lifts his head. "Romi, my heart," he whispers.

I stare into his fiery gaze, breathless with the rush of emotion and sensation spinning through me. Although I cannot speak, it feels as if we are communicating with our bodies.

You are mine as well, I say.

I will protect you, he returns.

And I, you.

On the heels of a breath, he angles his head to the side and claims my mouth in a devouring kiss. Our tongues tangle, and I'm grateful for the shelf behind me and his arm, strong around my waist, to keep me from collapsing to the floor.

Everything blurs into nothing but sensation. I catalog all of it —the way he tastes, the firm, sensual command of his mouth over mine, his strong body pressed against me, the muscled planes of his chest, the way his palm splays on my lower back.

He tugs at the ties of my shirt until it falls open. My aching breasts feel heavy, and my nipples are tight. We break apart, our breathing echoing in the air around us.

His eyes are like fire on mine. I feel the heat of his gaze when it dips down to my bare breasts. His hand slides down the side of my neck, the calloused surface of his touch like the sensation of sparks leaping over my skin. His hand is so big it engulfs my breast as he lightly cups one and then the other, teasing his thumb over my aching nipples.

I hear myself whimper, arching into his touch. As if he can read my thoughts, he knows I need more. He dips down and catches one nipple with his mouth. I cry out at the sharp, hot suction. He teases my nipples, and all the while, I barely recognize the sounds I'm making—pants, whimpers, moans.

I'm wearing what I typically wear for riding and working in the stables. A laced top over a riding skirt that falls to my knees with leggings underneath. My chest heaving, I feel restless and needy, desperate for something.

I can feel the hard, hot length of his arousal pressing against my lower belly. I know I want him to fill me. I'm near frantic for it. He lowers his head again, his eyes burning into mine.

"I need to taste you," he growls.

In answer, I drag my palm over the thick ridge of his arousal. I feel bold, unfettered, and entirely unafraid. He yanks at my leggings, shoving them down around my ankles before dragging my skirt up my thighs. He lifts me, and I feel the rough surface of the table against my bottom as he slides my hips onto it. I'm still wearing my boots, and my ankles are bound by my leggings. My knees fall open, and he steps back, his eyes dipping down. I feel my pussy clench. I'm so wet and slippery, aching for him to fill me.

Once again, I'm startled by my whimpering. His fingers tease through the wetness while my hips rock into his touch. He lifts his eyes to mine again.

"I cannot take you completely. Not now. We must wait," he says.

My breath is coming in sharp pants as I look at him and nod.

"But I can give you pleasure."

At that, he sinks two fingers inside me, and I cry out sharply. When he withdraws his touch, I'm startled to hear myself plead, "Thorne, please."

He swiftly unlaces his breeches. My eyes go wide at the sight of his thick, long shaft. A glistening bead of his seed rolls out the tip. He slides his big palm around my waist, splaying the base of my spine as he nudges me to the edge of the table, where my legs dangle down with my knees falling further open.

We watch together as he fists his thick cock and brings the tip of it to my slippery wet folds, smearing his seed all over me. It's beyond arousing. I can hardly bear the force of need pounding through me. I watch as he slides the thick crown up and down over my swollen bud. He draws back slightly, and I bite my lip to keep from moaning at the sight of his arousal dripping over me.

I've never felt like this. All I want is for him to fill me and make me plump with his alien baby. I was so pleased to be ignored by the men on earth, but now I want nothing more than

Thorne's complete attention. I want him to fuck me for days, to make me come again and again, to give him babies.

"You are mine," he whispers before claiming my mouth in another melting kiss.

With my breasts bare, my knees open, and my pussy begging for him, all I can do is whimper. He breaks away again, and we watch together while he smears more arousal all over my pussy before nesting the tip of his cock right in my entrance. I feel empty, and I want him to fill me. Yet he has complete control.

He holds still before shifting to slide the underside of his cock over the center of my pleasure. I feel myself spinning and tightening inside as sharp rays of pleasure streak through me. I tumble into it and shudder all over. While I'm still lost in my climax, he notches his tip at my entrance once again, barely stretching me, and I feel the heat of his release filling me.

When he pulls it out, my pussy is covered in his glistening, pearly seed. His eyes burn into mine. He lifts his fingers and brings them to my mouth.

"Taste us," he tells me.

———

Thorne is all I can think about over the following days. Our wedding cannot come soon enough. I'm so impatient for it that I don't even care how caught up Jane is in making sure I have a beautiful dress.

Thorne comes to see me again. And again. That supply room becomes a place of pleasure for me. When he's not with me, I walk in, and I remember what he has done with me. Simply thinking about it arouses me.

Chapter Seven

THORNE

"Thorne's not available until after his wedding and week of pleasure," Hunter teases with a sly wink.

Asher chuckles. "I've considered that. After you have a baby on the way, I'd like you and Hunter to go with the team for the princess."

The prince's eyes darken with a flash of anger. Ever since his princess was kidnapped while she was pregnant with their heir by a rebel faction on the other side of our peaceful, bountiful planet, anger doesn't even capture the depth of emotion he feels. Along with many of us.

It isn't just those of us who guard the royal family, but most of our planet's citizens. The royal family and our democracy have brought us great wealth and benevolence within the galaxy. A greedy, small group of noisy men is trying to destabilize it all. Time and again, the ugly parts of history play out on repeat. And just like on so many other planets, it is almost always a few unhappy men who create problems and try to drag everyone down with them. All because they want to feel more important.

They don't realize that true importance comes from recognizing one's place in the universe. We savor and revere women here because they give us life. They protect our very existence from the moment of our inception. Our choice to honor and revere them has elevated us and brought us nothing but goodness. We have a beautiful planet, so many resources, and enough largess to share with other less fortunate planets. Such as Earth, the very planet to which we turned after so many women died during the space storm that struck our planet.

"Things have quieted," I offer. "We know from earlier excursions that we have more to do to keep our people safe. They aren't going to go away. The king has told us as much. They think they gain more from stealing."

Hunter chimes in, "We think they have established an outpost in the mountains."

"They're not aware that we have communication and technology monitoring there," I add. "We don't have monitoring for security, but they set up equipment to monitor the wildlife."

Asher looks thoughtful as he taps two fingers on his chin. "Why don't we speak with the biology team at the university?" he muses. "It would be beneficial for them and us to collaborate on this."

"My mother will know who I can speak with," I offer. "She still teaches a few courses there. Her specialties are the plants we've brought from other planets in the galaxy. She will love this." My lips tug into a smile. My mother *will* love to have something to focus on. Since the loss of my father, she has felt betwixt and between.

Hunter nudges me with his shoulder. "Excellent idea."

Just then, there's a light tap on the door. "Yes?" Asher calls.

The door opens, and his princess, Jane, peers into his office. She's holding a baby, and her belly is already swollen with another.

Asher's eyes lock onto her. "Yes, my love?" he prompts.

"I heard Thorne is in here," Jane says as she approaches Asher.

He gives her a brushing kiss on her lips, and immediately lifts their son from her arms, nesting him in the crook of his elbow.

"You heard correctly," Asher teases with a grin as he gestures toward me.

Jane turns to me, resting her hands on her hips. "Are you ready?"

"Tomorrow can't come soon enough," I say.

My tone is light, but I mean it deeply and completely. I have gone to see Romi every day at the stables, and it's all I can do not to fully claim her while I wait for our wedding. Even then, I'm hopeful she's already with our child.

Jane's eyes narrow as she studies me. "Have you met with the tailor?" she asks.

"Of course," I insist. "You sent me a list, and I have attended to every task and appointment on that list."

Before I fell for Romi, I would've been more grudging about these tasks. Now, they are nothing. They are simply steps I have to take to seal my union with my beloved.

Jane's lips twitch, and I turn my head at the sound of snorting laughter. Both Hunter and Asher are chuckling at my state.

I shrug. "I mean what I say, quite literally. Tomorrow can't come soon enough."

Jane lets out a soft sigh, her eyes warm. "I'm so grateful you found Romi." She pauses. "Honestly, I'm surprised you didn't connect with her sooner. She's at the stables all the time."

Hunter rolls his eyes. "Thorne likes to ride when no one is around. His mount is kind of a jerk to anyone other than Thorne."

"Silver likes Romi," I chime in.

"Of course he does," Jane says. "She has the magic touch with horses. She was worried that she might have to leave if she didn't find a mate soon enough. Even though I assured her that would never happen, she still worried."

My heart twists. I don't like thinking of Romi worrying about something like that. At all. Although she is open and vulnerable with me, I can sense her guarded heart and know she's been hurt in the past.

"She needn't worry," Asher offers. "We need to do better when we recruit for mates to make sure they understand that. Even if they don't mate, they will be safe and we will not return them to Earth."

"There's a wrinkle in that plan," Hunter comments. "With the men from Earth here, they seem frustrated with our matchmaking service. They have plenty of women on Earth, and next to nothing to offer them."

"Except their tiny green zone," Asher says with a sneer. "And, without our planet's support, they would starve. They have another century before their planet might recover. I will keep talking with Kayden about security for the men visiting from Earth. I'm concerned they have something else in mind for their visit here."

Chapter Eight

THORNE

I'm standing at the front of the wedding room. It's not what humans would call a church, but it's similar. Our planet recognizes and honors all religions from all planets, but we also are deeply aware of not granting too much power to any religion. We worship all life and the bounty of the universe.

As I wait, I'm restless for Romi's arrival. Asher, Hunter, and Kayden are waiting with me. They are my closest friends and the men to whom I would turn for anything. They would lay their lives on the line for me, as I would for them. It's fitting for them to be with me for this ceremony.

Electricity sizzles through me when Romi enters the space. Her braided dark hair is twisted atop her head. Her angular features have an aristocratic quality to them. Her dark eyes lock with mine as she walks toward me. Unlike on Earth, women here are not given away in marriage. They give themselves freely.

Romi, my bride and my mate, stops in front of me. Her strength and fierce independence draw me to her. When her eyes meet mine, and I see the vulnerability flickering there, I want to wrap her in my embrace and protect her for all times.

A sensation that is becoming familiar to me, the tug on my

heart, as if there is a cord tying us together, hums. The connection is so powerful it can never be broken.

Romi's hands hold mine, and we speak our vows, promising and pledging ourselves to each other. The prince is presiding over the ceremony. For all his teasing over the past week, his gaze is entirely somber when I glance at him just before he dips his chin to pronounce us bound.

I know he understands how I feel. Relief washes through me when I can wrap Romi in my embrace and our lips meet. It feels as if a clap of thunder echoes around us. The reverberating force of our joining feels complete.

The next few hours pass in a blur for me. We leave the ceremony to walk with the crowd to the royal compound, where the prince and princess live along with the king and queen. The reception is outdoors with ample food, drink, and celebration in honor of our marriage and mating. At one point, I glance down at Romi, taking in her wide eyes and the tiny furrow between her brows.

I lean down to whisper in her ear, "How are you?"

Her lashes lift when she tips her face toward me. Her lips curl in a small smile. "I am well," she says. "But a little overwhelmed. It's a lot."

Lifting a hand, I trail my knuckles along her cheek. "It is. We can leave to go to our new home whenever you want."

"We can?"

The desire that sizzles under the surface whenever I'm near her burns a little hotter. "We've been here long enough. We've had our ceremony and been honored here. Trust me, we can go. Those who want to stay and enjoy the festivities don't need our presence for that."

Romi's teeth snag the corner of her bottom lip, and my entire body tightens. She takes a quick breath and lets out a little sigh. "Let's go then."

I glance around, catching Asher's gaze. He's seated across from us. I mouth, "We're leaving."

He nods in acknowledgment before leaning over to say something to Jane. A few moments later, they stand and discreetly organize the security team to escort us to our new home. I know where it is, but I haven't actually been inside yet. The grounds are nearby, though.

Romi's hand is warm in mine as we walk, flanked by the men and women who usually help me guard the royal family. A hum of desire buzzes through me. I know I will need to be gentle with Romi, to contain the primitive force of desire that runs through me like a rushing river whenever I'm near her. This is her first time, and I need to honor that.

When we reach the stone wall surrounding our new home, I lead her through the gate and close it behind us. There's a magnetic click once we step through.

Romi glances toward me. "Is it always closed?" she asks.

"When we're here," I say.

This woman, who has so thoroughly stolen my heart, who is so strong and brave with an independence that carries an edge of defiance to it, catches her breath. Her eyes widen as she glances around. "Is this really ours?"

Protectiveness surges through me, along with a sense of pride. This is our planet, where we take care of each other and the women here. I know she's seen the royal compound because she's lived in a house there for months now. I know she's also seen where her friends live in similar homes. Yet I love how surprised she appears.

"Yes. Did you expect anything less?

Her eyes hold a sheen of tears. "No, I just..." She lets out a quick breath.

Her eyes arc about our private grounds. It is, of course, much smaller than the royal grounds. But it's private, with lush flowers, fruit trees, and a well-tended vegetable garden.

"Come with me," I say, giving her hand a light tug as I begin to walk forward.

We follow the short path from our gates to our home, which

is a typical home for our area. Even for the royal family, we don't waste space. Here, we make things beautiful but economical. Most of the homes are single story and built to withstand the occasional space storms that blow across our planet. Every planet faces weather events throughout the galaxy.

We have learned in our travels over the centuries that planning for what we may face is the key to our survival. On this planet, we mostly get blasted by fierce winds and rains, so we keep our buildings sturdy. Beautiful and simple in design, they are also sustainable so as to not waste resources.

Romi's lips curl in a soft smile as we walk up the stone steps onto a wide porch with a roof. The home is built into a small hill to optimize power and heating during the cooler months.

The main area has a tall ceiling with windows offering plenty of light from our planet's sun, which burns brighter but softer than the sunshine on Earth. There's a comfortable sitting area with furniture facing a large stone fireplace. The kitchen is on the other side with a large island for seating. A hallway just beyond leads to three bedrooms and another room that could be a playroom for children or an office.

"Would you like a tour?" I ask.

At her nod, I simply swing my arm around in a circle in the main room before leading her by the hand to show her the bathroom off to the side of the kitchen, which also has laundry. We make our way down the hallway as I point out the rooms until we reach the door to our bedroom at the end. This leads into a suite, a large room with windows facing the front gardens and our own private porch area. The bed is set against the wall. The bathroom suite has a tub and shower and a large shared closet.

Romi peers into the closet, her eyes widening slightly to see the clothing for her.

"Jane took care of that," I say. "She had your clothes brought over from the house where you were staying, and your other friends helped select more from one of the clothing stores in town."

Romi presses her lips together. "I'm still not used to having more than one or two things to wear from Earth." She lets out a bemused laugh.

She walks back into our bedroom and spins in a small circle before approaching the windows. Just being in the bedroom causes my pulse to kick faster and faster, my need for her burning hotter with each passing second.

I stop behind her, resting my hands on her shoulders. Forcing myself to take a slow breath, I feel my shaft lengthening and hardening. This is how it always is with her, and I presume it always will be.

Stepping back slightly, she leans the back of her head into the curve of my shoulder. I let one hand slide down her side to wrap around her waist, resting on the soft curve of her belly.

There's no doubt she's aware of my arousal. She shifts back slightly, the motion nestling my cock between the curves of her lush bottom. I dip my head, my cheek resting against hers, as I dust a kiss along the side of her neck, savoring her sweet, slightly sharp scent. The sharpness is more on the surface of her personality, but underneath is the sweetness that she hides so well.

I can't help but nip lightly on her neck, nearly growling when she lets out a little whimper in the back of her throat. I rock my hips against her bottom, gratified when she shimmies against me.

I force myself to lift my head and take a slow breath. "I want you," I say, my voice gruff and frayed from the desire I can barely contain.

She turns in my arms, boldly dragging her palm over my shaft. "You know I want you. I want *all* of you."

I have to clench my teeth as I breathe her in. "I don't want to hurt you."

"You could never hurt me. I want you to fill me completely. Please," she whispers, leaning close and pressing a kiss just over my heart. I can feel the heat of her lips through the fabric of my shirt. It's like a brand on my skin. Her eyes are burning hot when she lifts her gaze to mine, once again boldly dragging her palm over my length.

My cock pulses under her touch. "Now," she says.

Chapter Nine

ROMI

Staring into Thorne's fiery golden gaze, I feel the heat of his arousal under my touch. Time today has felt like forever. It's everything I wanted—to pledge myself to him for all time, to promise to protect him, and to hear his promise and pledge to me.

Yet ever since that promise was made, all I can think about is finally having all of him. My heart is tangled within this infinity pulse. That connection with him is why my desire is so powerful. Quite simply, I need him. *Now.*

I'm dripping wet. I can feel my arousal on the insides of my thighs, and I feel empty, and I want him to fill me.

"Please," I whisper again.

He stares at me, seeming frozen. His eyes hold mine as he bends low and claims my mouth in a kiss. I lose myself in it, as I always do. Our tongues twine. It's a dance and a war. The war is a joint fight until we can find completion.

He breaks away, spinning me quickly toward the bed. My wedding dress buttons from top to bottom, and he hooks a finger where the top button is nestled between my breasts. He yanks it down swiftly. Buttons skitter across the floor as my dress falls open. I'm naked underneath. My nipples are tight, pink points, aching for him.

His gaze sweeps up and down, and my skin suffuses with heat. For a moment, I feel completely exposed because I'm almost bare while he's still fully clothed. But his reverent and hoarse voice spins around my heart.

"You are everything to me," he rasps.

His hands curl over my shoulders before he pushes the dress down, and it falls in a rumple at my feet.

"I will bring you your pleasure first," he murmurs.

All I can do is nod as his hands begin mapping my body. I lose myself in sensation. He is so big and strong. His big hands cup my breasts, teasing my nipples. I feel the sharp suction of his mouth on one nipple and then the other. His fingers tease into my slippery core, filling and stretching me before he slides my hips on the bed.

I fall back on my elbows as he pushes my knees apart, whispering, "Your pussy is beautiful. I love that it's so wet for me."

While my breath comes in ragged pants, he brings his mouth to my sex. I'm crying out as he fucks me with his fingers and his tongue. My orgasm hits me abruptly, in a noisy burst, and I cry out his name, a prayer on my lips.

Seconds later, he rises, and I sit up slightly because I need to see him. He strips down, and his skin is shimmering with gold light flashing. His tail flexes behind him, and I stare at his length, uncertain for the first time how he can fit inside me.

"I promise I'll be gentle," he says when my eyes lift to his.

His seed drips out of the tip onto my pussy as he stands in front of me. I want to taste him, so I do. Leaning forward, I slide my tongue over my lips and murmur, "Mmm," at the tangy, salty flavor.

"Do you want more?" he asks.

"Yes." I suck his length into my mouth.

I love the way the flavor breaks across my tongue. Even though I've never done this before, he seems to like everything I do. His fingers grip my hair tightly, the sting on my scalp welcome.

He praises, "Yes, Romi, you're perfect, my love."

I break free to look up at him, and he says, "I need to be inside you."

I shimmy back on the bed and spread my knees. His seed drips all over me, the sight deeply arousing. He curls one of his big palms around his thick length and smears it over my pussy, and we watch together.

"Look at me," he orders.

I lift my eyes to his. "I'm going to make you mine."

"Please," I whisper.

We watch together as he nestles his thick crown in my pink folds. He slowly begins to fill me, and I stretch around him. The pressure is intense, but between my arousal and his cum-covered shaft, there's very little friction. I feel when he reaches my barrier.

"Tell me if it hurts," he whispers.

My breath is heavy, and I see my swollen clit poking out as he keeps filling me. He breaks through my barrier, and my breath sucks in sharply for a moment.

"Look at me," he orders.

When I meet his eyes, his gaze feels like a caress. "Are you okay?" he asks.

I can't even speak because all I can feel is this rushing sensation, this feeling of completion that I've never experienced in my life. I nod.

On the heels of a shuddering breath, he seats himself fully inside me. He palms my cheek as his other hand slides around to press low on my back. He nudges me closer to the edge of the bed. My legs dangle down around him as he moves inside me in slow, deep pumps.

He withdraws, telling me, "Watch," and I see his thick length, glistening from his arousal and mine, sliding in and out of me. My own climax is upon me, and I'm begging him.

He reaches between us, his fingers teasing above where we're joined. I feel as if I'm scattering into a million pieces, the pleasure so intense I break apart. I hear him calling my name as the heat of his release fills me, and he holds me close as we tumble together.

Chapter Ten

THORNE

I'm still buried inside Romi as I hold her close against me. A sense of relief rolls through me on the heels of the most intense climax I've ever experienced. My body knows I'm finally where I belong. Here, joined with Romi.

She's soft against me, the feel of her warm skin and curves a contrast to my hardness. Her head is tucked into the curve of my neck. I can feel the soft gusts of her breath across my skin.

I slide a palm up her back to sift my fingers through the tendrils of her hair that dangles along her neck.

I feel her lift her head and drag my eyes open to meet her dark gaze. "I've never seen you with your hair down," I say, my voice a little hoarse.

Her lips curl into a lopsided smile. "I'm very practical. I don't usually wear my hair down," she says.

"I love how practical you are. You can leave it up if you'd like."

She reaches up with her hands and quickly takes out the pins holding the braid up. A moment later, she slides a single finger through to undo the braid. My breath hitches as her hair falls around her shoulders in a glorious, glossy tousle.

I trail my fingers through it, savoring the silky feel of her long locks. "You're beautiful. It's beautiful. I like it up or down," I murmur.

"You do?" She tips her head to the side, her eyes skeptical.

"I do. It's beautiful down, but I have better access to your neck when it's up." I lightly trace my knuckles along the side of her neck, gratified when I feel the goose bumps rise on her skin. "How are you feeling?" I ask.

"Better than I've ever felt." Her cheeks are a little pink with her reply.

Reluctantly, I withdraw from her. Because I know she may be sore. "Let's shower."

I help her off the bed, and we walk into our bathroom together, enjoying a shower under steaming hot water. Afterward, we both change into comfortable clothes and pad out to the kitchen.

"I can't believe it," she begins as she turns toward me. "But I'm hungry. I was so, well, overwhelmed with everything after our wedding that I actually didn't eat much."

"Jane made sure we have everything we need," I say.

Opening the refrigerator, I gesture toward a large tray of fruits and meats and other things. "And, of course, we have our communicators, and we can ask for anything to be delivered."

"Even with the gate locked?" she prompts.

When I nod, she shakes her head with a wondering laugh. "Even though I've been here a few months, I don't know if I'll ever get used to how well everyone is treated here."

"That is why we are a galaxy hub. We have ample resources to make sure everyone who is living, or visiting, on our planet has enough food. We pride ourselves on being one of the best planets in our galaxy. One of these days, I will have to take you to the food court where the station for all the ships is. I think they've been out of service since you were born, but it's like the old airports on Earth. They often had areas with a lot of food for travelers."

Romi's lips twitch in another smile. "I would love that. Sometimes I feel greedy. Something as simple as having lemonade is such a luxury. But for now, I just want to be with you."

My heart feels warm in my chest as I smile down at her. The connection between us feels as if it tightens. "We have an entire week to ourselves. Even if we get food delivered, we don't have to deal with anyone."

Reaching around her, I pull out the tray of snacks and gesture toward the pitcher of lemonade. "Jane obviously knows you're partial to lemonade," I tease lightly. The sound of Romi's giggle sends a fiery sizzle of need through me.

———

The days pass too swiftly for me. The morning before the end of our week alone, I come awake to the feel of Romi curled up against me. She's sleeping, but her hand rests on my abdomen. The moment my awareness flickers on, arousal slides through me.

I know that the desire will never weaken between us. It will always be like this. My lips curl into a slight smile. I sift my fingers through her hair, feeling when she comes awake.

Her voice is raspy, soft on the edges from her sleep when she speaks. "Good morning, Thorne," she whispers before tipping her head to the side and pressing a kiss on my chest.

My palm slides down over her bottom because I can't help it. I give her a little squeeze, savoring the soft give of her curves. "Good morning."

She moves her knee slightly in invitation, and I delve my fingers into her cleft to discover she's aroused, just as I am. Her palm slides down over my abdomen to drag over my length, and I already feel my seed rolling out the tip.

"Romi," I gasp when she tightens her grip and strokes up and down.

"Thorne," she murmurs before rising up and tossing the covers back.

Seconds later, she straddles me, and I shift back to sit up against the pillows. I want to wake up every day with a lapful of Romi.

She rocks her hips, her slippery folds nestling around the underside of my shaft. "I need you, Thorne," she says, bringing her hips up.

"I'm yours."

I notch myself at her entrance, savoring the feel of her slick, clenching channel as she slowly seats herself over me, sheathing me inside of the very heart of her.

I grip her hips, holding her still, as I grapple for purchase inside to keep from losing control instantly. She's impatient and lets out a little whimper.

"Easy, sweetheart," I murmur.

Her lashes lift, and her dark eyes lock with mine.

"We may not have every day together like this, but we are bound for all time," I whisper.

Once again, that link between us feels as if it's tightening when she leans closer and brushes her lips against mine. "I know," she whispers.

I feel her words on my lips as she brings her hips up and sinks over me. I'm filling her again and again, and we're both chasing our release. After days together, I know the song of her body. I know when she's quickening. She makes these little sounds in her throat and moves with restlessness.

Reaching between us, I tease my fingers over her slippery, swollen bud. She cries out, her channel clenching tightly around me and drawing my release out. My climax sizzles through me like a clap of thunder followed by a bolt of lightning.

I hold her close, knowing there will be a lifetime of this with her. Yet feeling a bittersweet sense that these days alone are about to end.

Chapter Eleven

ROMI

When couples mate on this planet, they have a week alone, no matter their stature in society. I marvel at this. Here, those with the least are treated better than the richest on Earth. There isn't such a thing as a class system here. Everyone is considered worthy of dignity and respect. Although it's a luxury, I also recognize the week of pleasure after a wedding is designed to enhance the likelihood of making babies.

On the very last morning, when Thorne fills me yet again, he leans close, whispering, "We have made a baby this week."

It's shocking that I even want this after years on Earth hoping to never give birth to a child. Over the days that followed, I could swear I'm pregnant. I've even convinced myself I know when the conception happened, but I haven't said a word about it to Thorne because I'm waiting to be sure. I think it was the very first time we were fully joined. I felt a quickening inside as if something had taken root in my body.

In the days after our week alone ends, our daily life settles into a comfortable rhythm. He goes to his job as part of the security detail for the royal family, while I go to my job at the stables to care for the horses. Every evening, we have dinner together, and I savor those mundane moments. I'm aware his job will take him away from me for travel at times, and I've made my peace with that. I'll miss him, but it's part of loving him, and I accept it.

Thorne comes to see me almost every day out at the stables. He spends time with me and his mount, Silver. Silver has a prickly and aloof personality but has become more comfortable with me and seeks me out daily. He's not a particularly affectionate horse, but he always nudges me with his nose, snorting a little as he passes me by when I'm out in the pasture.

Thorne also takes me almost daily in the supply room. He says it's our special place. I float through my days awash in pleasure. Of course, I also go home to him every night and lose myself with him yet again. It's strange to experience so much pleasure. I feel wanton and greedy with him, but I love it.

Nadine and I meet during one of her breaks at the cafe. I sip my tea, as does Nadine, who is expecting another baby soon. Trudy teases Nadine, and her cheeks go pink, but she shrugs with a small smile. "I've told Kayden this has to be our last baby. This will be our third, and I think that's enough."

Trudy nods. "You are somewhere where you have that choice, so be grateful."

At that moment, Trudy straightens her shoulders. Glancing around, I realize the queen has walked in with one of her close friends. She greets everyone kindly before she stops at the counter to order.

The queen turns to Nadine and me, her eyes lingering on me. "Marriage appears to be treating you well," she says with a dip of her chin.

I always feel flustered around the queen, but I gather my composure. "It does. I love this planet so much," I say, my words coming out in a rush. "Thank you so much for welcoming me here along with other women from Earth."

The queen's eyes crinkle at the corners with her warm smile. "Women from Earth are always welcome here, as are men. And we are grateful to those of you who have chosen to stay and help us rebuild because we lost so many women." She pauses, tilting her head to the side. "I sense you are with child."

Heat rises in my cheeks. She nods again as if to herself. "I think you know it. Jane has told you where to go for medical care?" she prompts.

"Oh, yes. She introduced me to the doctor a few days before my wedding. I have an appointment next week. I hope to find out before Thorne has to travel," I explain.

After the queen leaves, Nadine arches a knowing brow. "How does it feel?"

"How does what feel?" I hedge.

Nadine lets out a soft chuckle. "Being pregnant."

I take in a quick breath, letting it out in a rush. "I'm excited, and I can't believe it. When I was on Earth, the last thing I wanted was to end up pregnant. Here, I feel desperate to have Thorne's baby. I want to make a whole family with him."

Nadine reaches across the table to clasp my hands. "You will. Have you told Thorne you suspect you're pregnant?"

Chapter Twelve

ROMI

A week later, Thorne is with me at the doctor's appointment. "I'm never telling you again if I suspect I'm pregnant," I tell him.

Thorne slides his gaze to mine and shrugs. "I thought you were pregnant anyway."

Just then, there's a light knock on the door. I call out, "Come in!"

The doctor, a beautiful alien woman with purple skin and a tail, walks in. I liked her immediately when Jane introduced me to her. She has a practical, comforting manner to her. At the moment, I'm relieved she's here because Thorne has been driving me crazy with his protectiveness.

She glances from me to Thorne before her eyes shift back to me again. "He's being overprotective," she says matter-of-factly, quickly assessing the situation.

"Yes!" I exclaim. "Please tell him I'm fine."

She gives Thorne an understanding smile. "Your mate is healthy and likely to have a safe, healthy pregnancy."

Thorne shrugs. "I must take care of her." His jaw is clenched, and his features are drawn tight.

"You are ridiculous," I press. "I'm fine. Please, please relax."

The doctor checks me over and confirms my pregnancy. I have to ask her because I can't help it. "Is it safe to, um..." My cheeks are on fire. "You know, have sex?"

"Absolutely," she says with a shrug. "There are no concerns until about a week before you're due. Even then, you can still orgasm, but I would avoid penetration because you're so close to delivery at that point."

I'm seated on the examination table with paper crinkling under my legs. Thorne has already peppered her with questions, and he's sitting impatiently in a chair.

The doctor studies him, her eyes narrowing. "I'm writing you a prescription," she announces.

"For what?" His tone is sharp.

"To relax," she says.

His gaze softens. "I love Romi, and I want her to be safe at all times."

"We have the best healthcare in the galaxy," the doctor assures him. "She is safe and healthy."

After she leaves, I beckon him to me. He stands in front of the table. I should mention I'm naked under my gown, and it's rumpled around my waist. When he steps between my knees, I realize he's aroused.

My own arousal gushes onto the paper under my thighs. I mean to tell him something practical, like to relax or something like that. Instead, I say, "I need you."

The woman on Earth who never even wanted to have sex is now begging her husband. I crave the feel of his thick shaft filling me in the doctor's office.

Thorne doesn't hesitate. He swiftly frees his shaft, and I bite my lip to keep from moaning at the sight of his seed glistening as it rolls down his length.

Since I'm already naked under the gown, he spreads my knees, murmuring, "My good girl," before he fills me.

It's quick and dirty, and my cries are muffled in our kiss when

I feel the heat of his release pumping into me as my own climax shatters through me. Afterward, he cleans me up and helps me dress. His touch is careful and reverent, and I feel like a fragile gift he's protecting. The emotion that rises inside is so powerful I almost don't know how my heart can hold it.

Chapter Thirteen

THORNE

Cupping Romi's cheeks, I look deep into her eyes. "I love you," I murmur against her lips, my words, a promise, a tattoo on her heart.

"And I, you," she whispers.

I take the shape of those words and carve them into my soul. After giving her a lingering kiss, I straighten and force myself to step back. Curling my palm into a fist, I thump it lightly over my heart. "I will always carry you here while I travel," I tell her.

She presses two fingers to her lips and blows me a kiss. A moment later, I sit astride Silver. On a gust of air, I press my heels against his flanks. Silver breaks into a trot before lifting to fly low over the ground.

The others on the team traveling with me rendezvous in the air over the next few minutes. We travel for a full day to reach the far side of the planet. We are following the leads from the intelligence Hunter and I received about the use of this isolated area as a hidden place to plan. What the rebels don't know is that one of our university teams set up cameras here several years prior to monitor wildlife. When we got a report from a student about the activity here, we activated them for us to monitor.

As history spells out time and again, from galaxy to galaxy and planet to planet, events that lead to crises, such as the space storm that struck here a few years ago, can also lead to unrest. Once we got wind that this tiny but loud rebel faction wanted to essentially eliminate our peaceful democracy, we knew we had to pay closer attention. They claim they don't want to destroy our democracy. They claim they simply want the opportunity to change the royal succession. However, they are vocal about disagreeing with our people's reverence for women. They want to destroy our planet's strength that has come as a result of our peaceful, benevolent system that cares for everyone.

Over the ensuing time since we discovered their planning and since Princess Jane's kidnapping, we've taken steps to increase our monitoring. We don't want to interfere much at this point, other than to ensure safety if needed. We'd like to see how far they plan to go.

Hunter and I are the lead spies for the security team. During times of peace, not much is needed from us. But, of late, we've led the secret group on mission after mission to better understand how sophisticated the planning is within the rebel group. The kidnapping of our princess has shaken the leadership for our planet.

We land that evening on the outskirts, miles from the outpost and in the thick of a silver forest. We don't want to arrive by air because we don't want to be visible from a distance. Our horses lead us through the forest. This side of the planet is similar to parts of Earth, where the days are incredibly long during the warm season and much shorter and darker during the cold season.

Hunter and I have already set up a camp. Camp for us is fairly sophisticated in the sense that we have the equipment needed for shelters and all basic amenities. Once our team is secure in camp, we activate a security dome over the entire forest area, including where our mounts will roam while they are resting. Similar to horses on Earth, they need space to graze.

I glance over at Hunter at the small table where we sit. "Well? Any updates?" he asks.

I take a long swallow from my water and shake my head. "Raven communicated that he wanted to talk, so let's see if we can reach him now," I reply, referring to another team member who works remotely and often scouts ahead for us. I tap my communicator. "Raven?"

"Right here." His voice crackles a little. Our shield can sometimes affect the communicators.

"What's the update?" I ask.

"We monitored the cameras today, as usual. We did see alerts for activity from the rebels there. As predicted, based on our earlier recordings, your timing is perfect. They're there. However, there are more than we expected. What concerns me the most is they have some of the visitors from Earth with them," Raven explains.

Hunter and I both straighten in our chairs. "What?" I ask sharply.

Hunter's brows hitch up as his gaze meets mine from across the table.

"We're surprised and concerned too. We suspect that the men from Earth have somehow communicated with the rebels here," Raven replies.

"Well, we have info they've been present at one of the bars in the rebel's town," Hunter comments.

"Whether or not the men from Earth knew about the uprising here, they do now," Raven points out.

"The last thing we need is to stir this issue up further." I pinch the bridge of my nose. "The men from Earth are violating their agreement. No one can travel here and consort to act against our people," I say.

"Exactly," Raven replies. "You'll have to take them into custody and bring them back to the capital. We've already spoken with the queen and the king about it. They're all in agreement. Those men cannot remain here. Beyond arresting them and forcing them to leave the planet, we will consider reducing the supplies we send Earth and ask our other allies to do the same."

"I guess we know what we're doing tomorrow," Hunter says dryly.

"How many men are here?" I ask.

"As it stands, there are more of you than them. Three stragglers haven't been arrested from the protests and three men from Earth. You all have a twenty-man security detail," Raven says.

"Sure, we have more of us, but how will we transport them all back?" Hunter asks pointedly.

"We'll send transport," Raven chimes in. "Once you have them in custody, let us know, and one of our high-speed hovercraft can be there within a few hours."

I meet Hunter's eyes, and we nod in unison. "Okay, we have a plan," I say. "We'll update you tomorrow."

Later, as I try to fall asleep and get the rest I know my body needs, my mind spins to Romi. Hunter and my other friends have told me once you experience the infinity pulse, you can feel the connection when you're away, even from a distance. I had honestly doubted this until I met Romi. Even then, I wondered how I would feel all the way on the other side of our planet.

My doubts are kicked away now. There is no doubt I feel that connection. The pull is not as powerful as it is when I'm close to her, but its ever-present force pulses. I miss Romi. So very much.

Although I'm restless, I manage to fall asleep. I convince myself it's because Romi somehow knows I need the rest and soothes me through our connection.

———

The following day, the first part of our morning goes smoothly. We make our way to the rebel's outpost before they're awake.

We surround them with our horses and arrest them. The men from Earth are none too pleased.

"We are guests of your planet!" a man named Allen declares.

"You are," I agree. "But as a guest of our planet and an emissary from Earth, you must respect our laws. These men are rebels, all of them under investigation for trying to interfere with our democratic processes and overthrow our royal family."

One of the men from Earth sneers. "You look down on us, yet all of the goodness you have here came from what was first on Earth."

"Our planet has a wealth of resources, none of which Earth gave us. Earth *was* once a leader in technology, and we have adopted some of those methods. Your people destroyed your own environment and much of what you had because you didn't appreciate it. We have learned from your mistakes and improved upon anything we learned from your people. We love our planet. All of the beings who reside here honor our planet and our people. On Earth, you hate half of your population, and you treat your women like indentured servants."

Another man from Earth rolls his eyes. "I can't believe you worship women here. We can take our women back," he says.

"You cannot," Hunter says.

"What little supplies you humans have on Earth are gifted to you from our planet and others," I add. "You can travel freely amongst the galaxy. If you choose to interfere with the free choice of anyone in our galaxy, not just your planet, you will lose all support from us and our allies."

The man who appears to be the leader of this little ragtag group from Earth blanches. For they know that without the supplies from other planets, they will not survive. As it is, they're barely surviving, from what we can tell. They don't distribute their supplies evenly, which worsens the unrest among the people there.

One of the rebels finally speaks, "There may be more of them than us, but they can't transport us."

Our hovercraft appears on the horizon as if on cue, landing a short distance away on a flat grassy area. There's grumbling and muttering before we begin to load everyone up.

Just as it's about all over, one of the men from Earth makes a run for it, and I take chase. Unfortunately for him, he stumbles off the edge of a cliff.

"Oh, for fuck's sake," I mutter to myself.

Chapter Fourteen

THORNE

As much as I want to leave him to the slow death he assuredly deserves, we treat everyone with decency here. When I hear the sound of his cry, I know he is alive, so I must get him help.

I return to the group, reporting to Hunter, "I will go rescue him, but I don't want to delay the departure."

"I can stay back with you," Hunter offers.

Hunter waits with me, along with Raven, who arrived with the hovercraft. In addition to his duties for the royal security team, he is a healer.

"Perfect. If this guy has any injuries, you can help," I say.

The others leave, the hovercraft departing with the prisoners first, followed by the rest of our security group leaving on their mounts. Hunter, Raven, and I make our way back to the ledge where the man fell.

We peer over the edge of the cliff. Our mounts are waiting impatiently. Part of me wants to fly down, but it's too rocky and there's nowhere to land.

"We're gonna have to do this the old-fashioned way," Raven says with a rakish grin.

I've always liked Raven. Bright and quick-witted, he thinks on his feet and never hesitates to simply act. In short order, we agree I will repel down to the man because my climbing skills are the strongest. Hunter will fly down on his mount and hover in the air nearby in case something goes awry.

A while later, once I reach the man, it's clear he will survive, but he's groaning in pain. He eyes me skeptically.

"I don't want to go back to Earth," he says.

"So you jumped off a cliff to stop that?" I counter.

"Yes. I'll give you all the information you want. I'm a spy on Earth. You can confirm it with the authorities there. The other men I traveled here with have been communicating with the protesters on your planet. That's why we planned this trip. The leadership on Earth is changing."

The man winces when he tries to move. "We'll talk more once you're safe," I say.

I quickly prep him to be carried up on the climbing ropes. A few minutes later, I'm making my way back up the cliff with Raven guiding us by rope and Hunter keeping an eye out along the way. Once we're safe, Raven sets to work, taking care of the man's injuries. His name is Jack.

All of this takes long enough that we figure it's best for us to wait for another hovercraft to come back the following day. We communicate that to Kayden and the prince, who assure us a small hovercraft will arrive at daybreak tomorrow.

This time, we make ourselves comfortable in the outpost and gather more information from Jack. Earth has been in the throes of an oppressive and frankly stupid regime for centuries. The desperate decisions they've chosen have been made worse by the lack of resources.

"There are good people on Earth," Jack says. "They would like to give women their rights back. They would like to cooperate with other planets in the galaxy so that we can repair our planet and use the new technology available to survive better. These men heard about the rumors up here and decided, I guess"—he rolls his eyes at this—"to come here, a place that's amazing, and make it shitty like Earth." He shakes his head.

"Even the men are miserable there because the women hate them. It's just…" He circles his hand in the air. "Quite literally, a stupid and vicious circle."

The building we're in rattles from a gust of wind. I open one of the windows to see a massive storm rolling in over the mountains.

I take a breath. "Looks like we might be here for more than a day."

Jack glances between us. "What do you mean?"

"On this side of the planet, storms usually last at least a full day, and they're fierce," Hunter explains.

"Don't worry, we're safe," I add. "This outpost is built into a mountain. If the wind gets too bad, we have shelter deeper in the mountain. We'll just wait it out. We have enough food and supplies for our planet's full army to live here for an entire year."

"For the three of us, we're good to go," Hunter chimes in.

Jack looks between us, letting out a wondering laugh. "And the fighters on Earth are made to fight for nothing. God, we're so stupid."

Hunter chuckles. "Disaster makes people desperate, and desperate people don't always make smart and strategic choices. It's a scramble for control."

We wake the following morning with the storm still raging. We're not even able to communicate. Our remote cameras do work, though, because those lines are impervious to the poor weather. The team tells us via video feed that they will return once the storm ends.

I miss Romi, and it's obvious Hunter misses Melody. Once again, I feel the tug in my heart. I silently tell her I love her and will be safe. I feel worry reverberating through the line.

Chapter Fifteen

ROMI

When we go to meet the returning security team, Hunter and Thorne are not with them. I look at Melody and see my own anxiety and fear reflected in her eyes.

"What does this mean?" I ask the prince a short while later.

We know there are prisoners because we watched them being escorted off the hovercraft, along with some of the men from Earth. It's a shock yet not at all surprising to those of us from Earth. We know what the men from Earth are capable of.

"One of the men from Earth tried to make a run for it," the prince explains. "Hunter, Thorne, and Raven stayed back to rescue him and get him medical treatment. We were planning to send a ship to them in the morning since the man from Arthur is fairly injured, and although Raven has done his best, we need him to be here at the hospital."

Melody throws her hands up. "I don't care about the man from Earth. Men from Earth are simply cruel. Why didn't they just leave him?"

The prince nods, and Jane presses her lips into a line. I can see her disappointment.

"We know they're cruel to women, but our planet treats even criminals well, so we will treat them well. But the delay in their return is because a storm has blown in on that side of the planet, and those usually last for a full day. There's a reason there are no towns over on that side of the planet—it is our storm side," the prince explains.

"When it rains here, it's only for a few hours or maybe a day," I burst out.

Jane stands, reaching for my hand and one of Nadine's. She squeezes us both. "They are safe. Asher has assured me that they are staying in the outpost there and have enough supplies and food for the entire army—for our whole planet—for over a year. They will be safe, and as soon as the storm is over, we'll go get them."

Jane's touch is comforting, but I'm afraid. I miss my mate, and I could swear that even our baby misses our mate. I slide my palm over my belly, which is round now. It's startling to have a baby grow so fast.

I reach for Melody's hand and squeeze it. "They're going to be okay," I tell her, almost as if I'm trying to convince myself.

"I promise you that I will report any updates as soon as I receive them," Asher says, dipping his head solemnly. "You have my word. If you have questions at any time, just communicate with Jane, and she will get me immediately. I don't care if you wake me in the middle of the night. I will get an update at any time. We know the patterns on the storm side. This should be over in another day or so."

"Is this the kind of storm that killed so many women?" I ask.

Asher nods. "Yes, but we don't live on the storm side, and the women's festival doesn't happen on the storm side. It is on that side of the planet, but closer to that area. The storm that blew through didn't last twenty-four hours, but it was brutal and fierce—what we call a once-in-a-century event. We can control many things, but the weather is not one of them."

"Thank you," I finally say. "I appreciate you keeping us informed, telling us everything."

"Are our people safe here with these men from Earth?"

Asher is quiet for a beat before he nods. "Yes. We are gathering information, but we think that the rebels here—which exist on every planet, not just ours—convinced the men from Earth that there were more of them and that they had more power here than they do. I think the men from Earth regret their choices deeply, and they will be sent back to Earth and likely never be allowed to visit this planet again."

Melody lets out a quick sigh, and I squeeze her hand again.

"I understand," she says. "I'm just worried. I want Hunter safe."

"They will be safe. They are safe," Jane assures us.

I hold her words in my mind as Melody and I depart together. We go to my place because she and Hunter's child is currently with their nanny. Like me, she's distressed and tells me she wants to vent without upsetting her child.

After we arrive, I wave for her to sit down on the couch and get her a glass of her favorite juice. She loves lemonade, but I know she's partial to a juice native to our new planet. It is sweet with a sharp tang to it. I love it as well, but I still prefer lemonade.

Once we're seated in my living room, Melody looks around, her lips curling into a soft smile. "It's like our house but a little different."

My gaze arcs about the room before my eyes meet hers again. "I will never stop being amazed to live here. Everything here is beautiful and wonderful, and I'm just—'" I let out a deep sigh, so relieved to be off Earth.

I feel tears spring to my eyes, and when I meet Melody's gaze again, I can tell she knows exactly how I'm feeling. Living in fear all the time is exhausting, and it wears you down to where you feel like you lose parts of yourself in the process.

"They'll be okay, right?" I ask.

Melody takes a breath and a sip from her drink. "I believe they will, but I don't know. One of those storms killed a bunch of women. That's why we're here."

"Yes, but they were out in the open. Thorne and Hunter are safe inside," I say quickly. "The prince explained they can go into the mountain. They have housing and food." My voice rises, and I realize I'm trying to convince myself as much as her.

"Do you want to stay with me tonight?" she asks a few moments later.

"Like a slumber party?" I tease slightly.

"Yes. You can stay in our guest room. I promise our baby sleeps well, and it'll just be nice not to be alone while we worry. We can watch shows," she says.

Those of us who originally arrived here from Earth have started watching old television shows that played on Earth before the planet turned into a baked desert. The luxury on those shows is beyond what I could even imagine. I've seen some old pictures, here and there, of the relics of Earth's glory, but it's shocking how much was lost.

They're from what the history books here tell us was Earth's heyday after the Second World War. Then television came out, and the seventies, eighties, into the nineties and early two-thousands are show after show of people living what appear to be utterly ridiculous lives of luxury. We've learned so much about our own history since arriving here. We're allowed to sit in on any of the classes here, so we've done so out of curiosity. The rich people on Earth before its ruin were ridiculous. They even had what they called reality shows with these women called housewives. Being a housewife on Earth now is nothing more than pure drudgery.

"Let's," I say, grinning at her.

I end up staying with her for four nights, and we still haven't heard word from Hunter and Thorne. On the fourth morning, I wake and roll over, feeling a stronger tug on the cord that makes me believe I'm connected to Thorne even though he's on the other side of the planet.

I hurry out to the kitchen to find Melody making coffee.

"I'm going to the other side of the planet. I'm going to find them," I tell Melody.

Her eyes go wide. "Romi, you're pregnant. You're due in two weeks."

"I know, but the prince said the storm was over, and we still haven't heard."

When Melody falls quiet, I know what she's thinking. "You can't just go like that. You have to tell them you're doing this."

Within an hour, I'm standing in the prince's office.

Asher studies me. "They aren't all the way on the other side of the planet, and I was going to call you down to tell you this morning. Our hovercraft went to pick them up, and they're fine. Except they hit a dust storm on the way back and crash-landed. I'm not thrilled with you going to do this, but I sense you're going to do it whether I agree or not."

I lift my chin. "I am." I might be trembling inside, but I cling to my defiance for strength.

"Well then, the queen is going to lead a rescue mission. You can go with her," he says.

"In another hovercraft?"

The prince narrows his eyes. "You must be safe for me. Thorne would literally do me harm if he knew I'd let you do something reckless. The queen has an entire fighting team at her disposal. They are trained to do things like this. Go with them."

There's a sharp knock on his door, and it opens before he can even speak. It's the queen.

Her eyes lock with mine. "Romi. Come with us," she says.

The next span of time passes swiftly. Before I know it, I'm on one of these hovercrafts for the first time. We're zooming across the planet, and I'm marveling because it is so shockingly beautiful from above—the mountains, the lush trees, and the beautiful silvery lakes. All of it takes my breath away.

Yet, all the while, I feel the cord—my connection with Thorne—becoming stronger and stronger as we travel.

"He's hurt," I say, shifting to look at the queen, who sits calmly beside me.

"Perhaps. But they have communicated with us, and Raven is a healer. He will keep him stable," she says, her tone confident.

"What if Raven is hurt?" I burst out.

"If Raven is hurt, they will all take care of each other. We have heard from them. They are all alive."

She leans over, reaching for both of my hands. Her touch is soothing and warm. I feel she is conveying her strength into me as she holds on. "I would not lie to you. I would never have brought you with me, with our team, if I thought you would encounter your mate in a state where he could not be saved." She gives my hands one last firm squeeze before releasing them and straightening. "We're almost there."

She stands and strides to stop between the chairs of the two women flying the small craft. Although I've been a woman my entire life, I'm so accustomed to women being ignored and discounted—never given opportunities to be in charge. Women are just as intelligent as men and far less likely to let their pride or ego get in the way, yet it's still discombobulating to see women handling entire missions like this. There is not a man among us.

The queen and the princess have explained to me that their women fighters are just as elite as men. They recognize that men may have more physical strength due to their size, but that's more of a brute type of force. Women's strengths are different, and they offer different gifts.

Before I know it, we're landing, and I can see the other hovercraft tilted on its side in a pile of sand. My heart flies into my throat, and emotion rushes through me. I'm impatient to get out, find Thorne, and assure myself he is okay. I will not be able to relax until I know that.

Yet I defer to the queen. Because I'm a reasonable person, I wait impatiently. Once we disembark from the hovercraft, we discover they are all safe—but they are also all injured.

Raven is in the best shape and has done what he could, but he is limping badly.

The infinity pulse vibrates in my chest, and I follow it to find Thorne resting against the far side of the hovercraft.

He meets my eyes. "My love," he says. "Why are you here?" He instantly looks concerned as his gaze sweeps over me.

Chapter Sixteen

ROMI

"I'm fine. The doctor cleared my travel, and I'm here with the queen. *You* are the one who is hurt." I drop to my knees in the sand beside Thorne. I run my hands over him as if I can assure myself he's all better.

"Romi," he says, catching my hands with his. "I'm safe. I'm here. It was a dust storm, nothing more. It's over."

Tears roll down my cheeks, and he swipes them away with his thumbs, cupping my face before drawing me close and giving me a lingering kiss.

"How badly are you injured?" I demand when I gather myself a moment later.

A voice I don't recognize comes from behind. "He's bruised up pretty badly. I've done all the emergency medical care I can. He cracked some ribs and twisted his tail badly, which is more of a nuisance, but it hurts like hell."

Thorne lets out an annoyed huff. "It *does*." He gestures to the alien cowboy. "This is Raven. He is part of our security team and a healer."

"We need to get him back to our main medical facility. They'll have him in working order in no time," Raven tells me.

Although I'm worried, I'm so relieved to be back with

Thorne that the relief overwhelms my concern. I hold tight to his hand, fussing over him as the queen's team quickly gets everyone into the ship. Some of the women on the ship are experts at repairing things and will stay to repair the hovercraft and bring it back in a few hours.

"Minus the dents!" one of the women calls as we get ready to depart.

I've taken a liking to her. Her name is Trina, and she's tiny and fierce, with a sharp purple tail that twitches when she smiles. She tells me she's an *alien cowgirl*, which I think is hysterical. I'm surprised I haven't met her before, but she explains that she keeps to herself at home—although she's curious about the horses from Earth and wants to ride them. We've already made plans for her to do so.

When we get back to our town, my heart relaxes. I realize I've never felt this way about a place before. The closest I came was when my mother was still alive because I loved her so and felt safe when she was near. But even then, it was *her*, not the place.

Here, it's different. It's the place and the people. Thorne, Jane, Nadine, Melody, and their mates. Trudy at the coffee shop. The flower shop. The king and queen. The prince. They *all* matter to me. They've made their presence in my life something meaningful. They've created a sense of community I've never experienced before. With that community comes a sense of safety and protection. Ever since I mated with Thorne, that sense of protection has eased the anxiety that has thrummed inside me for as long as I can remember.

At the medical center, I can tell Thorne doesn't like being fussed over. He wants to be strong. To be *okay*. But all of them have to be cleared—including Raven. Raven had done some emergency stitches on himself for an injury in his side, but the medical team decided they needed to open it up and clean it properly.

He's frustrated, but he goes along with it, flashing a grin at the queen. "My queen, I will be fine."

She rolls her eyes. "I *know* you will, Raven. You always are."

She glances at me and laughs softly. "He's like another son to me. We have Asher, but his parents were our closest friends before they passed, and we have always doted on him. He is a funny boy—a sly one. He hides the depth of his heart behind his jokes."

When Thorne is finally cleared to leave, he reaches for my hand. "I just want to go home, love."

"I've already arranged for one of the local transport services to take us home," I say.

Thorne meets my gaze, rolling his eyes. "You *can't* be serious. I can walk. Also, where is Silver and the rest of our mounts?"

"They already picked them up. Your horses got back before you all did." I smirk. "I'm still in a huff about that."

When we get home, the moment we step inside, I can *feel* Thorne's relief. He sits down on the couch and reaches for my hand. When I sit beside him, he curls toward me, smoothing his palm over my belly and whispering, "How is our baby girl?"

"She's strong and healthy. Just like you."

I lean closer, and he gives me a lingering kiss. When he slides his hand down over my thigh and hooks his fingers on the edge of my dress, I sigh with relief.

Even I have taken to wearing dresses—they're so comfortable. And now, with my pregnancy, I like the loose, soft fabric. I savor the touch of his palm on my bare skin, but when he brings his fingers to tease between my thighs, I murmur, "Thorne, you need to rest."

"But I *want* you, love," he protests. "And I asked the doctor —she came to see me while we were at the medical center. She says I can still have you."

When he starts dusting kisses along the side of my neck, my body shivers, telling him just how much I want him. And of course, I'm *dripping* for him because it feels like it's been too long. Because it *has* been too long.

He is gentle, guiding me to straddle him right there on the couch. He fills me in slow, deep strokes, murmuring, "I love you, Romi. I missed you. You are my heart. You are my mate."

The moment he says that, my orgasm crashes through me, scattering pleasure like the sun inside me. I *savor* the feel of him, his release filling me as he holds me close.

That night, we fall asleep together, his palm resting on my belly as he whispers once more, "I will always come home to you. I will always love you."

Chapter Seventeen

THORNE

The wind gusts as my mount comes to a landing. Silver slows quickly, his wings tucking in before he comes to a complete stop. I dismount swiftly, tapping my communicator as I jog across the field.

Asher's voice comes through instantly. "I already sent them. You should see them in a minute," he says. "Romi went into labor early."

I freeze mid-step, my heart pounding. "She's not dangerously early," Asher reassures me. "I've already been given multiple updates as I flew back into the protected skies above our town. The medical team has kept Jane informed, and she's with Romi at the hospital. She promises me everyone is healthy and safe."

"Everyone?" I practically yelp.

Asher chuckles. "Yes. Romi and your daughter are safe and healthy."

My heart pounds so hard it feels like it might break a rib. Just as I reach the gate to the area, I spot one of the medical crafts waiting alongside one of the princess's personal transports. I ensure the gate is locked behind me and leap onto the craft. As far as I'm concerned, they can't move fast enough. I'm impatient even though I know they're flying as fast as they safely can through town on the way to the hospital.

Moments later, we arrive, and I jump off before the craft has even fully stopped, earning a warm-hearted rebuke from the driver. "Easy there," he calls over his shoulder. "And congratulations, by the way."

"Thank you!" I toss back as I sprint toward the entrance of the medical facility. I skid to a stop at the reception desk, barely able to catch my breath.

The receptionist looks up, smiling warmly. "Yes?"

"Romi—she went into labor early," I gasp.

"Oh, yes." Her smile remains steady. "The princess is with her. Room at the end of the hall."

I don't even know how long it's been since I spoke to Asher. Time has lost all meaning. I won't settle until I'm beside my mate.

I feel the pull of our bond tightening with every step. Just as I'm about to lift my hand to knock on the door, it swings open.

Jane smiles warmly. "You're here." She grabs my hand, pulling me inside before pressing a finger to her lips. "Shhh. She's resting. I'll be right outside."

Romi is asleep, propped comfortably against the pillows, our daughter resting in her arms. My heart is in my throat, emotions slamming into me so hard it feels like I might break apart from the force of them. The protectiveness rising within me is stronger than anything I've ever felt—and considering I've spent my life as a bodyguard and a spy, that's saying something.

Our little girl is perfect; her tiny body curls against her mother's with her small, shimmering blue tail tucked around her hips.

Romi's lashes flutter, her lips curving into a soft, tired smile as she sees me. "You're here."

"I am."

"We didn't expect her today." She shifts slightly, tapping a button on the side of the bed so it lifts her up a little more. "It was so fast—" she starts, but the door opens, and her doctor enters.

The doctor glances between Romi, our baby, and me. "As I mentioned earlier, human women from Earth often have slightly different gestation periods here. It's not an exact science. Romi, you seem to have an even shorter one than most, but your baby is completely healthy."

I swallow hard. "And Romi?"

The doctor nods. "She's very healthy. The labor was quick."

I shake my head. "I tried to get back in time."

Romi's tone is dry as she replies, "I think it's best you didn't. You would've been so stressed out, it would've been a problem."

The doctor chuckles. "Perhaps."

I watch as Romi shifts, adjusting our daughter against her. She's already nursed, and everything looks peaceful.

The doctor asks me, "Would you like to hold her?"

Before I can even process it, Romi is handing her to me. She is so tiny, so perfect, and suddenly, I'm afraid. I've never held a newborn before—especially not *my* newborn.

But the moment she's in my arms, everything else fades away. She blinks up at me, and her dark eyes—so like Romi's—stare into mine with an intensity that steals my breath. I could swear she already knows me.

The doctor watches as I hold our daughter like she's the most fragile being in the universe. And to me, in this moment, she is.

Her little tail twitches against my thigh, and she lets out a tiny sound, curling her fists before stretching her hands open and nuzzling against me.

I swallow hard, my voice rough. "I think she wants to nurse."

Romi reaches for her, and I watch, mesmerized, as she adjusts our daughter against her, guiding her to latch. It's the most intimate, powerful thing I've ever witnessed. The love I feel in this moment is bigger than I can even contain in my heart.

"Do you have any questions before I leave you two?" the doctor asks.

I try to focus, taking a shaky, unsteady breath. "I—uh, I hope not. Is there anything I need to know about feeding her or anything like that?"

"She's nursing well, as you can see," the doctor assures me. "My main advice is to make sure Mama gets plenty of rest. Within the week, the support nanny agency will reach out to help keep the house clean, take care of errands—anything needed so Mama and baby can rest and stay healthy."

She checks in with Romi as I stare down at our little girl. Her tiny eyes blink open, and my heart lurches.

The doctor leaves, and Romi asks, "How are you?"

I glance at her, feeling the sting of tears in my eyes. "Just glad you're okay. That *she's* okay. I can't believe she's here."

"Are you ready to go home?" Romi asks.

"Whenever you are," I say. Then, softer, I admit, "I'm nervous."

The responsibility of caring for an actual child suddenly slams into me. However, I remain calm. We have a week together to adjust to it, and then we can decide how much support we want from the nannies.

Standing beside the bed, I'm looking down when our little girl's eyes open. My chest is suddenly tight again as she stares at me. Her gaze is solemn and intent, just as Romi's is.

Watching Romi with our daughter is nearly overwhelming. I couldn't have imagined it before, but somehow, our infinity pulse feels even stronger.

Chapter Eighteen

THORNE

The following day

Romi is curled up on the couch, cradling our baby in her arms. I walk over and hand her a cup of her favorite tea, the warmth of our home surrounding us. The sense of completion I feel is staggering. I have a family now. *We* are a family now.

The medical team has already checked in on Romi and our baby. A nanny arrived earlier to introduce himself and discuss scheduling options.

Romi sighs. "I love our baby, but I already miss work. I miss my horses."

I chuckle, wrapping my arms around her shoulders and pressing a kiss to her temple. "You think?"

She tilts her head, smirking. "A day or two a week, I can handle. But after that, I'll be stir-crazy."

"Whatever you want, I'll support," I say simply.

Her lips curl as she leans up to kiss me. "I'm so glad I'm here," she whispers.

I hold her close, our daughter resting peacefully in her arms. "You were meant to be here. It was our fate."

Chapter Nineteen

ROMI

One Year Later

I'm standing in the aisle between the stalls for the horses from Earth. I knew these horses well before they were transported to this new planet. Even though we don't speak the same language, I know they love it here. They have fresh water, ample feed, and more space to roam. In a way, my experience is a lot like theirs. For the first time in my entire life, I'm not scrambling to simply live with fear and threats barely held at bay. More than that, I feel loved and fulfilled in a way I could never have imagined when I lived on Earth.

It's late afternoon and almost time for me to leave work. One thing that hasn't changed since I moved here is that my job doesn't really feel like a job. I loved my job there, and I love it here. Here, I have the joy of learning how to deal with hybrid horses descended from ancient dragons and Earth horses. They are mostly like horses—if a bit more stubborn and a little snooty.

I take one last look around, pleased to see all the horses happily eating their evening supply of hay and milling about quietly. I was recently promoted to managing the stables and the grounds here, and I have a young woman who comes in the evenings to let them out for the night.

As I turn to leave, I glance down reflexively at my round belly. I'm pregnant with our second baby. Our baby's not due for another month. My doctor shortened her estimate this time because she thinks I will deliver early again.

While walking down the aisle toward the supply room to fetch my jacket, I feel that familiar pull when Thorne is near—his closeness creates a tingling sensation in my body and an intense sense of yearning.

He appears at the end of the aisle, slipping through the doors and approaching me with slow, deliberate strides. I stop by the door to the supply room—a mundane room, yet so full of meaning. It remains Thorne's favorite place to take me, and I sense that's what he's about to do.

He stops in front of me, his golden eyes narrowing. "Hello, my love," he says.

The low rumble of his voice reverberates through my body, and my knees go wobbly. As always, my body's response to him is powerful and instantaneous.

"Hi, my love," I reply softly, having long since given up feeling ridiculous about being affectionate with my husband, my mate, my fate—it's just the effect he has on me.

Thorne's eyes dip down, and he reaches out, sliding his big palm over my belly. "I love how you look pregnant," he murmurs.

When his eyes lift to meet mine, I feel weak, almost dizzy with need for him. His hand drops away, and he reaches past me to push open the door into the supply room. A moment later, the door clicks shut behind him, and I hear the sound of the lock engaging. It's not as if anyone would appear unexpectedly, but Thorne always locks that door. The sound is like a match thrown into the raging fire inside me.

Despite my practical needs when working, I don't ride when I'm this far along in my pregnancy, so I've mostly been wearing the loose, flowing dresses I've grown to love here. They're simply more comfortable, especially when I'm pregnant.

His hands slide down my hips. "How was your day?" he

murmurs as he bends low and nips the side of my neck. I shiver all over, arching into his touch like a purring cat.

"It was good," I say between pants and moans. "How was yours?"

"I missed you all day." When he lifts his head and his heavy, laden gaze meets mine, my heart thumps hard and fast in my chest.

"You say that every day, Thorne," I tease lightly, trailing a fingertip along the rugged line of his jaw and down his neck. His tail twitches, and I bite my lip, trying to contain the desire rampaging through me.

He lets out a low growl. "I need you now."

"I'm yours."

He spins me around, and I rest my elbows on a nearby table. His hands slide down my sides, curving over my belly and then down around my hips. When I feel the press of his hard length against my bottom, I push back into it, wiggling in invitation.

The cool air strikes my heated skin as he lifts my dress, the contrast only amping up the sensations coursing through me. I'm not wearing any panties—I almost never do. I could never have imagined this version of myself before I came here and before I met Thorne. Because when he's here, I know that when I see him, I will want him, and he will want me. As a result, we need to make it as easy as possible to give in to that desire.

He drapes my dress around my hips, and I savor the feel of the calloused surface of his palms as they curve over my bottom. "My love," he praises me as I arch my bottom up a little more and step my feet farther apart.

He teases me, his touch gliding over my bottom and up my thighs but never quite touching me where I want it. Impatiently, I feel my desire build, and I demand, "Thorne, I need you."

His chuckle is a whisper on the back of my neck. He sinks

two fingers inside me—I'm already wet, already ready. "I love you," he says softly, his tone patient and urgent at once.

I hear him moving swiftly, then I feel the hot brush of his arousal on my skin—a subtle, electrifying touch. I bite my lip, finally letting out a deep moan of satisfaction as he fills me slowly. Whenever we have sex while I'm pregnant, I feel so cared for. He's gentle in a way he usually isn't, and I love the sense of connection between us. He nudges into me fully, slowly rocking deeper and deeper, and I push back into him.

"Please... I need..." My voice breaks, and he pumps a little deeper as I rock back to meet him.

"That's my good girl," he murmurs.

Even though I'm pregnant at this moment, I feel fertile—an elemental force—whenever we're together, and I'm full with child like this. He withdraws, and I feel his seed dripping down over me before he sinks inside me again and reaches around. He knows exactly what I need. He knows how to touch me, to tease my plump clit until pleasure breaks over me. I cry out, clamping down around his thick length, savoring the feel of his release filling me.

He curls around me, staying inside as he dusts kisses on my neck. We slowly disentangle, and he helps me tidy up before we begin walking together back to our home. Our little girl is waiting at home with her favorite nanny and squeals when she sees us together. Thorne scoops her up and spins her in the air before showering her face with kisses.

I have come to love so much of this life—and yes, I absolutely love being adored and worshiped by my husband. But beyond that, I love the mundane evenings when we put her to bed and relax together, just cuddling and talking about our days. I love watching him clean up in the kitchen after he makes dinner for me. And I love falling asleep beside him, resting against his strong body while his tail curls around and holds me close.

EPILOGUE

Risa

The rain lashes me, striking my cheeks with stinging drops. I duck my head, wishing for a little shelter. I keep moving, counting my steps and *dashing* through the darkness until I reach the old horse barn. I push through the doors into the quiet shadows.

Once I'm inside, I let out a sigh. My breath is coming in heaves. I feel my way along the edge of the wall and push through another door into what used to be the feed room. It's only here where I feel safe turning on a light. I don't even know if anyone other than me knows there's still power to this old barn.

Pushing the hood back on my battered rain jacket, I shrug out of it and shake the water to the floor. Even though this kind of rain isn't particularly pleasant, Earth hasn't had rainstorms in decades. For the past few weeks, we've been having them in bursts.

People are rejoicing, thinking maybe the tide is turning—maybe our planet is going to get better again. Maybe we can grow more of our own food.

Meanwhile, I just want to leave.

My gaze arcs around this tiny room. Months ago, the

woman who used to feed and care for the horses had them all transported off the planet somehow. I used to help her. And even though I understood why she took them with her when she left, I miss the horses. They were the one bright light in my life.

I sink my hips to the floor and let out a sigh before reaching for the one piece of technology I have—the one thing Earth has clung to. I tap the screen to open it and skim through *Galaxy-Cosmo*, our social media, our only source of news.

My message box has a notification—unusual. I tap on it.

Let's meet.

I don't hesitate. I stand, reaching for the rain jacket I've never needed until recently. It isn't even mine. My grandmother had it, and I dug it out of her closet in her vacant, empty home. When the roof blew off a few years ago, I lost the one place I had to live.

When I step outside, there's no more rain. Just wind now. I hurry through the darkness into one of the—if you can call it that—fancy apartment buildings in town.

Minutes later, my friend Lena is letting me in. Her blue eyes are bright, her blond hair swinging in a ponytail. "Come in, come in," she says.

I walk in, glancing around in surprise. Lena, Jenny, and Martha are all here.

"What's going on?" I ask.

"There's rain. Finally," Jenny says.

I glance over. "Well, yeah, but why are we meeting tonight?"

"There's one of those matchmaker recruitment meetings for the other planet tomorrow. I say we go," Lena says.

"Oh, you mean, no matter what?" I prompt.

———

The following day, the rain is long gone, and the sun is beating down as I walk to the building where they've been holding these interviews for over a year now. I don't care whether I find a mate —I just want to escape Earth.

This isn't some glamorous, exciting story where we fight on behalf of Earth. We just want women to have better lives. If I end up marrying an alien space cowboy, so be it. But if not, hopefully, I can get them to see they have to attach some conditions to the help they give Earth.

Aphroditea is the richest planet in the galaxy. They spread their wealth amongst the planets, and Earth is the stepchild no one wants to deal with anymore. Earth was once powerful and led so many advancements for the galaxy. But while other planets took those advancements and made better worlds, Earth has destroyed its own.

As there always is for these interviews, there's a line. While I'm waiting, I see Lena waiting a ways behind me and wave to her, along with Jenny and Martha. Before I know it, I'm seated at a plastic table and a woman named Jane is smiling at me.

"You're a princess?" I ask, unable to hide the skepticism in my voice.

She rolls her eyes a little as she nods. "I am. That's how I ended up there. I actually think it would be great for you to come, but I'm a little worried."

"About what?" I try to keep the sharpness out of my voice.

"Do you actually *want* to go?" she presses.

I startle myself when I feel a tear slide down my cheek. Clearing my throat, I blink quickly—only to send more tears splashing onto my cheeks.

Jane reaches over, her hands curling around both of mine. "You're leaving with us in an hour."

Improbable as it is, Lena and I are both selected, which means Jenny and Martha will try to sneak onto the ship. When it was just me taking the risk, I was ready. Now, I'm fretting.

Although only four women are selected—which I learn is the maximum they take on any trip—the ship is busy with activity before we depart. It's a transport ship for goods and food for

Earth. They're even bringing back more horses, taken from another area on Earth. There's also a tense exchange as some men from Earth are being returned from the other planet.

When I finally step onto the spaceship, I almost can't believe how basic it is. It's a utilitarian space.

I've never left Earth. You have to be very wealthy to travel off Earth, and I am *definitely* not that.

I feel an unfamiliar sensation inside me, a sense of awareness chasing over the surface of my skin, an almost visceral feeling followed by a tug, right in the center of my chest. I glance around.

Lena smiles at me where she's seated beside a woman named Helena who gave us a bunch of information. Of the other two women selected, one of them looks exhausted, her eye terribly swollen and cheek bruised. The other is absolutely beautiful and looks utterly terrified.

The prince is sitting beside Jane, the princess. The way he looks at her makes me feel like I've walked in on a deeply private moment.

There are several alien cowboys on the ship. They're all tall, with tails, and despite their imposing presence—larger than the biggest human men I've ever encountered, and I wouldn't dare cross them in a fight. But there's a *protective* quality to them.

When my eyes finally drift to the front of the spaceship, I see a regal-looking woman in one seat and a man in the other. The second my eyes land on that man, I don't understand it, but I *know* he and I are connected.

His head whips around, his golden eyes locking onto mine. It feels as if there's an electrical force linking us together, shimmering between us. Heat rises, swift and overwhelming, blasting me from head to toe.

I feel like I'm about to go up in smoke.

RAVEN

I'm usually a focused man. So when I feel the hair rise on the back of my neck and my skin prickle with a sensation of electricity and heat, it's unsettling.

Glancing over my shoulder, my eyes lock with those of a woman. A *human* woman who's just boarded our spaceship to go to our planet and find a mate. She's dressed in practical clothing, a worn blouse and a pair of pants that are probably older than she is. Auburn hair. Bright green eyes.

I cannot look away from her. In the moment she blinks, I *know*. We are meant for each other.

Standing, I cross the short distance between us. There's a low murmur of activity around us as the crew readies the ship to leave. I am the lead pilot and shouldn't be standing here, feet away from this woman.

I notice the dusting of freckles on her cheeks, like a shimmer of gold, the way her eyes tip at the corners like those of a cat. Like Earth, our planet has cats. I suppose cats must be truly universal. They're too independent to be anything other than that.

I take one more step closer—only about two feet separating us now—and it feels as if heat engulfs me from head to toe. Her presence is intense.

The woman studies me, her green eyes narrowing. "Don't you have something else to do?" Her tone is sharp.

"Oh, I do," I say, rising to meet the dare in her gaze. "I just wanted to say one thing."

Her nostrils flare as she draws in a sharp breath. I savor the sight of the pink flush rising on her cheeks.

It feels as if the air around us is sparking. I wouldn't be surprised if actual smoke rose from the heat created by our connection.

"I'm Raven," I murmur. "And you've already met your match."

"My *match*?" she repeats, eyes flashing. "What do you mean?"

Thank you for reading Thorne & Romi's story - I hope you loved it!

If you'd like a glimpse from their future, you can join my newsletter to receive an exclusive scene.

Sign up here: https://BookHip.com/RTGPZWX

Sign up for my newsletter, so you can receive information about upcoming new releases & deals: https://phoebebelle.com/

Phoebe Belle lives on Earth. She loves escaping into happily-ever-afters, her family - human, canine and maybe even alien (not willing to rule that out because you never know!) - coffee and cooking.

https://phoebebelle.com/

facebook.com/phoebebellegalaxyromance

instagram.com/phoebebellegalaxyromance

www.ingramcontent.com/pod-product-compliance
Lightning Source LLC
Chambersburg PA
CBHW071439300726
48976CB00004B/1382